D0368858

Barbie™
STAR LIGHT ADVENTURE

THE SECRET OF THE GEMS

PAPERCUTZ
NEW YORK

BARBIE STAR LIGHT ADVENTURE "The Secret of the Gems"
Tini Howard – Writer
Jules Rivera – Artist
Matt Herms – Colorist (cover)
Matteo Baldrighi and Jules Rivera – Colorists
Cardinal Rae – Letterer

Dawn Guzzo – Design/Production
Sasha Kimiatek – Production Coordinator
Bethany Bryan – Editor
Jeff Whitman – Assistant Managing Editor
Jim Salicrup
Editor-in-Chief

ISBN: 978-1-62991-610-1 paperback edition
ISBN: 978-1-62991-611-8 hardcover edition

Papercutz books may be purchased for business or promotional use.
For information on bulk purchases please contact Macmillan Corporate
and Premium Sales Department at (800) 221-7945 x5442.

Printed in China
February 2017 by Toppan Leefung Printing Limited

Distributed by Macmillan
First Printing

IN ORBIT OUTSIDE BARBIE'S HOME PLANET OF PARA-DEN.
BARBIE, YOUR FRIENDS ARE GONNA *LOVE* PARA-DEN! I CAN'T WAIT FOR YOU TO GET HERE.
WE'LL SEE YOU SOON, DAD.
I'M JUST READY TO *RELAX*.
KING CONSTANTINE IS GREAT, BUT HE'S *VERY* SERIOUS ABOUT TRAINING!
...AND THE CASTLE ISN'T THE *BEST* PLACE TO PRACTICE MY SWEET JUMPS.
GOOD LEADERSHIP IS A LOT MORE THAN JUST LOOKING NICE IN FANCY CLOTHES, RIGHT, PRINCE LEO?
SO I HEAR!

...AAAAND LANDING COURSE IS SET! VACATION IMMINENT.

PARA-DEN IS THE *PERFECT* VACATION PLACE!

PLACES TO HOVERBOARD...
...OPEN FIELDS FOR PILOTING TRICKS...
AND PLENTY OF--
...BRIGHTLY COLORED FOLIAGE?
...GREAT VIEWS FROM UP HIGH?

HAHA, YES! HOW'D YOU GUESS?
WHAT ELSE--
--WOULD GET US SO EXCITED?

OKAY, EVERYONE. HOLD TIGHT. WE'RE COMING IN FOR A LANDING!

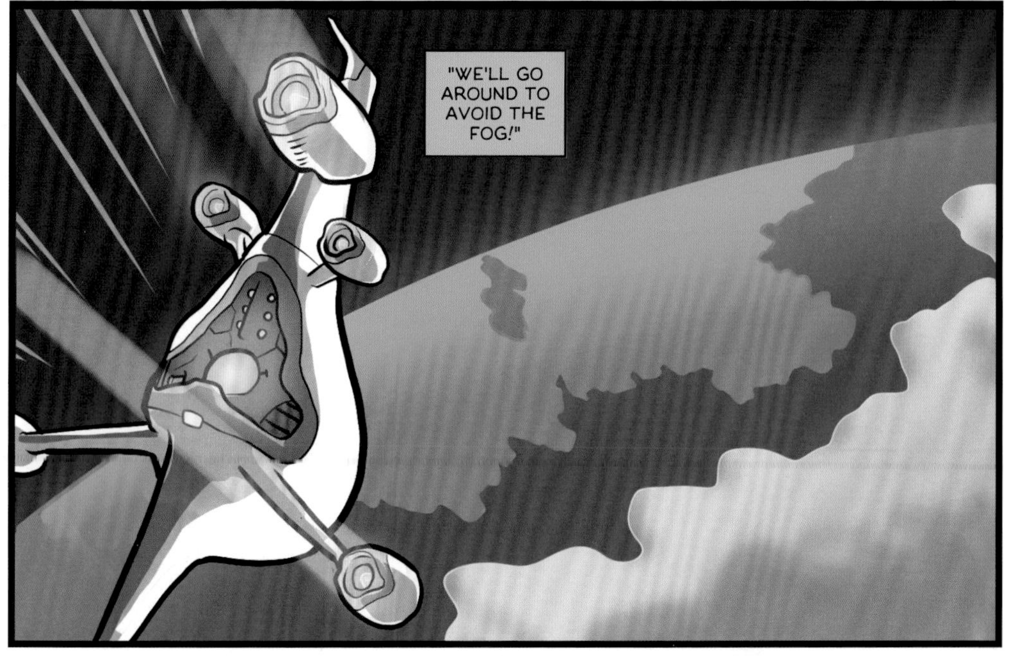
"WE'LL GO AROUND TO AVOID THE FOG!"

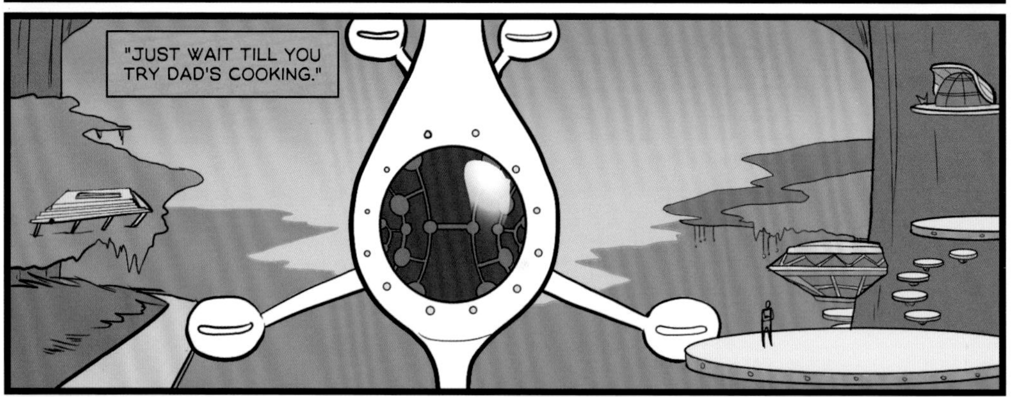
"JUST WAIT TILL YOU TRY DAD'S COOKING."

WHEN WE'RE ALL DONE EATING...

...WE'LL BE FULLER THAN THE MOON!

MMMM! SOUNDS AMAZING!
THUNK

WELCOME HOME, PRINCESS.
I *MISSED* THIS!

WE MISSED YOU, TOO, BARBIE. I CAN'T WAIT TO HEAR ABOUT ALL OF YOUR ADVENTURES.

NOW THAT WE'RE ALL ON THE GROUND, REMIND ME OF EVERYONE'S NAMES?
YEP! DAD, YOU REMEMBER...

"SAL-LEE, A HOVERBOARD RACING *LEGEND*...
HI THERE!

"SHEENA AND KAREENA, WHO ARE GRAVITY *GENIUSES*...
PLEASED TO--
--MEET YOU!

"AND LEO, BOTH PRINCE AND PILOT!"
CHARMED.

AND YOU'RE ALL ABOUT TO EXPERIENCE MY DAD'S **AMAZING** COOKING FIRST HAND! HE'S THE BEST IN THIS GALAXY...OR ANY OTHER.

THAT'S GOOD NEWS!
GURRRGLE

I COULD GO FOR A HOME-COOKED MEAL!

WELL, COME ON IN, I'VE BEEN COOKING ALL DAY!

GEMBERRY CASSEROLE, POMEGRANATE SALAD, BLACK BEAN TENDERS...

GALACTIMANGO PUNCH *FLOATS*, FIREFLY PIE, AAAAND NACHOS!

DIG IN!
ER, DAD...

WE WERE ALL *REALLY* EXCITED TO EXPLORE PARA-DEN. MAYBE...WE COULD MAKE IT A PICNIC?

THAT'S A ***GREAT*** IDEA! I JUST GOT A NEW BLANKET! FOOD'S BETTER OUT IN NATURE!

PHEW! I WAS GONNA HAVE TO HOVERBOARD IN THE HALL IF I DIDN'T GET OUTSIDE SOON. SHIPS MAKE ME STIR-CRAZY!

WOW, LOTS OF--
--ANIMALS OUT TODAY!
OH, YEAH! PARA-DEN'S ALWAYS FULL OF WILDLIFE.

OOOOOH!
PRRRRRRR

AWWWWWW!
CHEEP CHEEP
CHEEP CHEEP

WOW, BARBIE! I HAD NO IDEA PARA-DEN HAD SO MUCH GOING ON!

OH, YEAH! AROUND HERE, YOU NEVER KNOW WHAT YOU'LL--

--SEE!?
WHAT HAPPENED TO THE FOREST?
THE FOG HAS BEEN SO BAD, I COULDN'T SEE A THING! I CAME HERE ON MY WALK JUST LAST WEEK! I DIDN'T SEE ANYTHING.
HEY, AREN'T THERE SUPPOSED TO BE TREES HERE?

VROOOM
BEEP
BEEP
CRASH

I GREW UP IN THIS FOREST. I RODE MY FIRST HOVERBOARD HERE!

I GOTTA STOP THIS.

HEY!

HEY! HEY, YOU. YOU HAVE TO STOP!
WELL, WHAT ARE WE WAITING FOR? LET'S HELP BARBIE SAVE THE FOREST!

I *GOT* THIS.

HEY THERE! ANYONE HUNGRY?

AM I EVER!

COME AND GET IT!
I'M TRYING!
SHEENA, KAREENA, DO YOUR THING, GIRLS!
ALREADY--
--ON IT!
WHAT THE--!?
HEY!
JINGLE JINGLE
LET'S GET--
--THAT KEY!

SSHINK

COOL, IT WORKED! WE'LL BRING 'EM BACK, OKAY!?

WE'RE DOING ALL WE CAN TO STOP STELLAR INDUSTRIES, BUT...

URRROOOOOOMM
RRRRRRRUUMMMMMM

STOOOOOOOOOOOP!

SCREEEEECH
HEY, WHAT'S GOING ON HERE?
WHO'S THAT?!
PLEASE STOP CUTTING THESE TREES DOWN! THIS FOREST IS TOO IMPORTANT!
ACCORDING TO WHOM?

WELL, PEOPLE LIKE ME! AND THE ANIMALS THAT LIVE HERE! THIS FOREST IS AN IMPORTANT PART OF PARA-DEN'S ECOSYSTEM!
I'M SORRY, MISS. THAT'S WHAT WE WERE HIRED FOR!

WELL, SHE GIVES YOU NEW ORDERS! THAT'S PRINCESS STARLIGHT YOU'RE TALKING TO!
OH! OH, YEAH. THAT'S A GOOD POINT.
YES, I AM PRINCESS STARLIGHT, AND THIS IS MY FRIEND, PRINCE LEO. I'M SURE WE CAN DISCUSS THIS AND COME TO A SOLUTION.
RIGHT?!
?!
LOOK, KIDS. I UNDERSTAND YOU WANNA SAVE THE FOREST, AND THAT'S REAL SPECIAL. BUT WE WERE HIRED TO BE HERE.
I SUGGEST YOU TALK TO THE PERSON WHO HIRED US--MISS ELLA STELLAR.
ELLA STELLAR
STELLAR INDUSTRIES

"...SHE JUST MOVED IN!"
I *WILL* THEN!
DON'T WORRY, GUYS. WE'LL GET THIS ALL SORTED OUT!
NO ONE TAKES AWAY THE HOMES OF MY FRIENDS--

--ANIMAL OR OTHERWISE!

YOU MUST BE BARBIE!
HELLO, ELLA. THE CONSTRUCTION WORKERS MUST HAVE TOLD YOU I WAS COMING...?
THEY SAID YOU HAD A PROBLEM WITH WHAT WAS GOING ON IN THE FOREST?

WE ALL DID, MS. STELLAR.
I CAN'T UNDERSTAND WHY SOMEONE WOULD MOVE TO PARA-DEN, JUST TO CUT DOWN OUR BEAUTIFUL TREES AND DIG UP OUR GROUND!
I SEE. COME WITH ME, BARBIE. PERHAPS I CAN EXPLAIN.

VOILÀ, BARBIE! INTRODUCING MY ***STELLARSHIP!*** FEATURING STELLAR TRAVEL, POWERED ONLY BY *PARA-GEMS!*
PARA-GEMS? IS *THAT* WHAT YOU'RE DIGGING FOR OUT THERE?
PARA-GEMS ARE ONE OF THE GALAXY'S FASTEST FUELS! WITH *PARA-GEMS*, MY NEW STELLARSHIP BUSINESS CAN BRING THOUSANDS OF TOURISTS TO PARA-DEN IN THE BLINK OF AN EYE!
FIG 11
IT'LL PUT THIS QUAINT, QUIET LITTLE PLANET ON THE GALACTIC TOURISM MAP!
BUT...THE FOREST! SOME OF US LIVE THERE!

OH, BARBIE, YOU'RE A SMART GIRL. PEOPLE DON'T LIVE IN TREES!
WELL, I DO! AND THE ANIMALS DO!
OH. DO THEY HAVE A CONTRACT?
NO...?
WELL, I DO! YOUR LEADERS ARE IN AGREEMENT, AND THE LAND WAS PAID FOR FAIR AND SQUARE.
BUT... MS. STELLAR...
WITH RESPECT, MA'AM, WHERE DO YOU EXPECT THE ANIMALS TO GO?

"...THAT'S BUSINESS FOR YOU."
THIS ISN'T FAIR...THAT'S THE ANIMALS' HOME! WHERE WILL THEY GO NOW?

SQUAWK
HUH?!

SQUAWK
SQUAWK
OKAY, EVERYBODY...
BRRR
EE EEE

BARBIE TRIES TO CALM THE ANIMALS...
STAY CALM, PLEASE!

...BUT IT DOESN'T GO SO WELL.
YOU HEARD HER, EVERYONE. SINGLE FILE!

I'M NOT SURE THIS IS WORKING, BARBIE!

HEY, YOU! CALM DOWN!

SHEENA AND KAREENA TRY TO PROTECT SOME OF THE SMALLER, MORE HELPLESS ANIMALS.
WHERE DID THOSE--
--CHAMELEONS GO?

THERE!

COME BACK HERE!

BARBIE? I THINK--
--WE GOT 'EM!

PHEW!

THIS IS EXACTLY WHAT I MEAN!

I DON'T KNOW, BARBIE--
--WE'RE HAVING FUN!
BOING BOING BOING

THIS IS FUN FOR NOW, BUT THESE ANIMALS NEED A HOME.

WHOA!

YOU'RE SURE WE CAN'T KEEP THEM AS PETS, BARBIE?
NOT FOREVER. BUT MAYBE FOR NOW...
ALL RIGHT, EVERYONE. LET'S ALL MEET UP BACK AT DAD'S HOUSE, OKAY?

EVERYONE?

EVERYONE!
BARBIE...

I'M REALLY GLAD THAT YOU WANT TO PROTECT YOUR ANIMAL FRIENDS, BUT...

I'M NOT SURE OUR BACK YARD MAKES A GOOD HOME FOR ALL THESE ANIMALS.

AND ELLA STELLAR'S PROJECT IS JUST GOING TO KEEP EXPANDING.

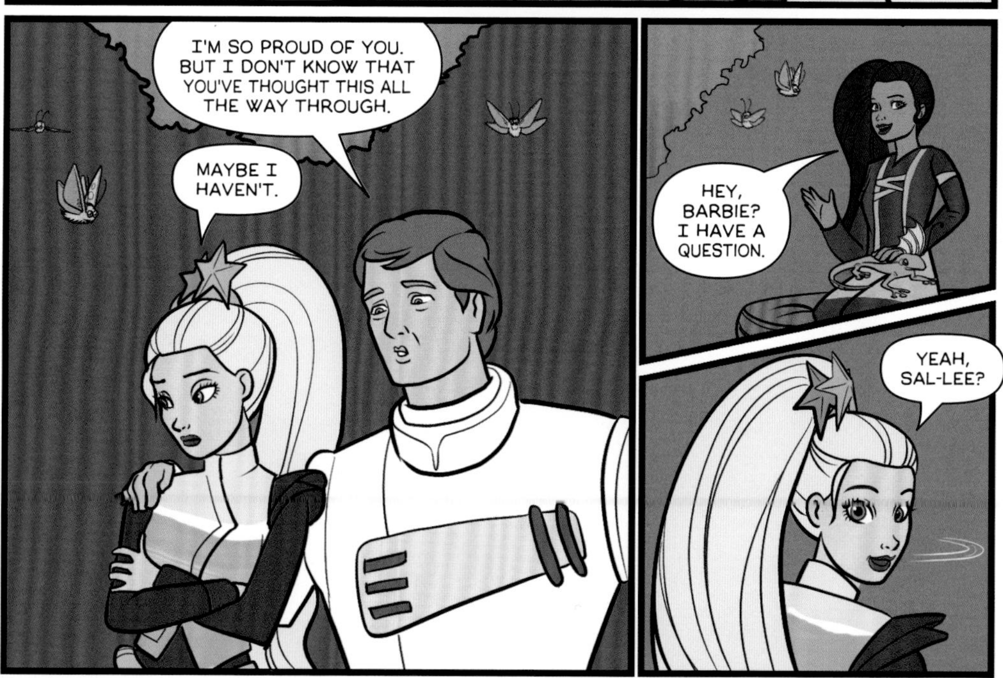
I'M SO PROUD OF YOU. BUT I DON'T KNOW THAT YOU'VE THOUGHT THIS ALL THE WAY THROUGH.
MAYBE I HAVEN'T.
HEY, BARBIE? I HAVE A QUESTION.
YEAH, SAL-LEE?

MAYBE I'M A CITY GIRL AND I DON'T GET IT. WHAT'S SO WRONG WITH THE STELLARSHIPS? THEY'LL BRING TOURISTS HERE. THAT'S GOOD FOR PARA-DEN.

WE'LL HAVE STUFF TO DO WHEN WE VISIT, YOU KNOW? AND THERE WILL BE JOBS FOR PEOPLE.

PEOPLE NEED PLACES TO LIVE, TOO.

SIGH
YOU'RE RIGHT. CITIES AREN'T ALL BAD.

THEY HAVE MUSEUMS AND FUN PLACES TO EAT. THEY GIVE PEOPLE PLACES TO LIVE, WORK, AND RAISE FAMILIES.

BUT A BEAUTIFUL PLACE LIKE THIS IS SPECIAL. IT'S THE HOME OF SO MANY ANIMALS, AND PEOPLE WHO LIVE IN HARMONY WITH THEM. THE FOREST IS BEAUTIFUL, BUT WE CAN ALSO STUDY THE LIFE-SAVING PLANTS THAT LIVE THERE AND ANIMALS WHO CAN TEACH US ABOUT OUR OWN PLANET!

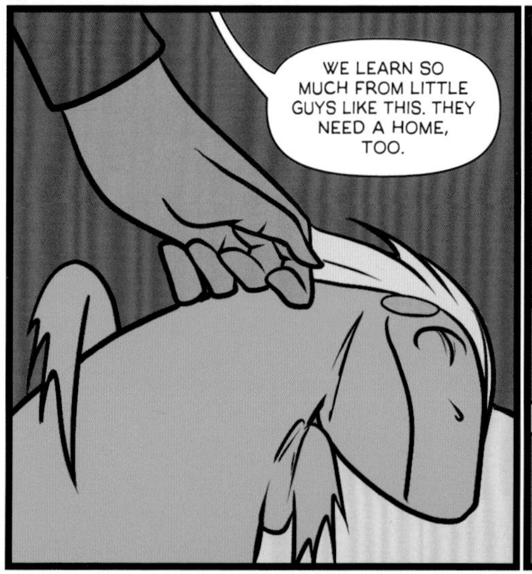
WE LEARN SO MUCH FROM LITTLE GUYS LIKE THIS. THEY NEED A HOME, TOO.

YEAH, I GUESS THEY DO.
SO, HOW DO WE GET *THEIR* HOME BACK? AND STOP STELLAR INDUSTRIES?

MAYBE...

WE JUST TAKE THEM THERE!

C'MON!

NOW.
SHHHH!

SAL-LEE, YOU
GO ON AHEAD!

EXCUSE ME, WORKERS? YOU'LL WANT TO MOVE. THERE'S AN ANIMAL STAMPEDE COMING!
HEY, YOU'RE NOT MS. STELLAR!
DEFINITELY NOT.
I'M NOT KIDDING! YOU MIGHT THINK I AM, BUT THEY'LL BE HERE ANY MINUTE!
HMM. WE'D GET TO LEAVE WORK EARLY FOR AN ANIMAL STAMPEDE.
GOOD POINT. LET'S GET OUTTA HERE!
READY?
LET'S GO!

OKAY, EVERYONE...

WELCOME HOME!

SQUAWK
SQUAWK
HAAAHAAHAHA HAAAHAHA... HAHAH...AH
EE EEE EE EEE

THIS ISN'T RIGHT. THIS ISN'T ANY KIND OF HOME FOR AN ANIMAL. THEY CAN'T LIVE IN CRANES AND BULLDOZERS!

...AND AS LONG AS I REIGN AS PRINCESS STARLIGHT, INNOCENT CREATURES WILL NOT BE FORCED FROM THEIR HOMES!
YEAH!
DOES...ANYONE ELSE HEAR THAT?
HONK HONNNNNK

WHAT... IN THE NAME--?!

--IS *GOING ON* HERE?!
MS. STELLAR! UH...*ER*, I CAN EXPLAIN!

STELLAR INDUSTRIES CAN'T BE ALLOWED TO FORCE ANIMALS OUT OF THEIR HOMES ANY LONGER!
SO...

YOU HAD YOUR ANIMAL FRIENDS RUN ALL AROUND MY *WORK SITE?!*

THIS IS GOING TO PUT US BEHIND PRODUCTION FOR *MONTHS!*

WELL, WE THOUGHT THAT BY SLOWING THINGS DOWN WE HAVE TIME TO DISCUSS A SOLUTION...

BESIDES, BARBIE IS SAVING PARA-DEN!

FROM *YOUR* EVIL PLAN TO STEAL ALL OF THE PARA-GEMS!

STEAL?!

NO!
AACKK!

I HAVEN'T STOLEN ***ANYTHING!*** THIS LAND WAS BOUGHT AND PAID FOR!

THE COUNCIL OF PARA-DEN WAS HAPPY TO SELL ME THIS LAND, BARBIE. THEY LIKE WHAT I'M DOING FOR YOUR PLANET!

MESSAGE FOR YOU, BARBIE. FROM THE HIGH COUNCIL OF PARA-DEN.

OH, NO...

DON'T WORRY, BARBIE!

I'M NOT WORRIED ABOUT BEING IN TROUBLE WITH THE COUNCIL, BUT I AM WORRIED ABOUT THE ANIMALS.
YOU DID WHAT YOU THOUGHT WAS THE RIGHT THING, BARBIE. YOU ALWAYS DO.

BARBIE?

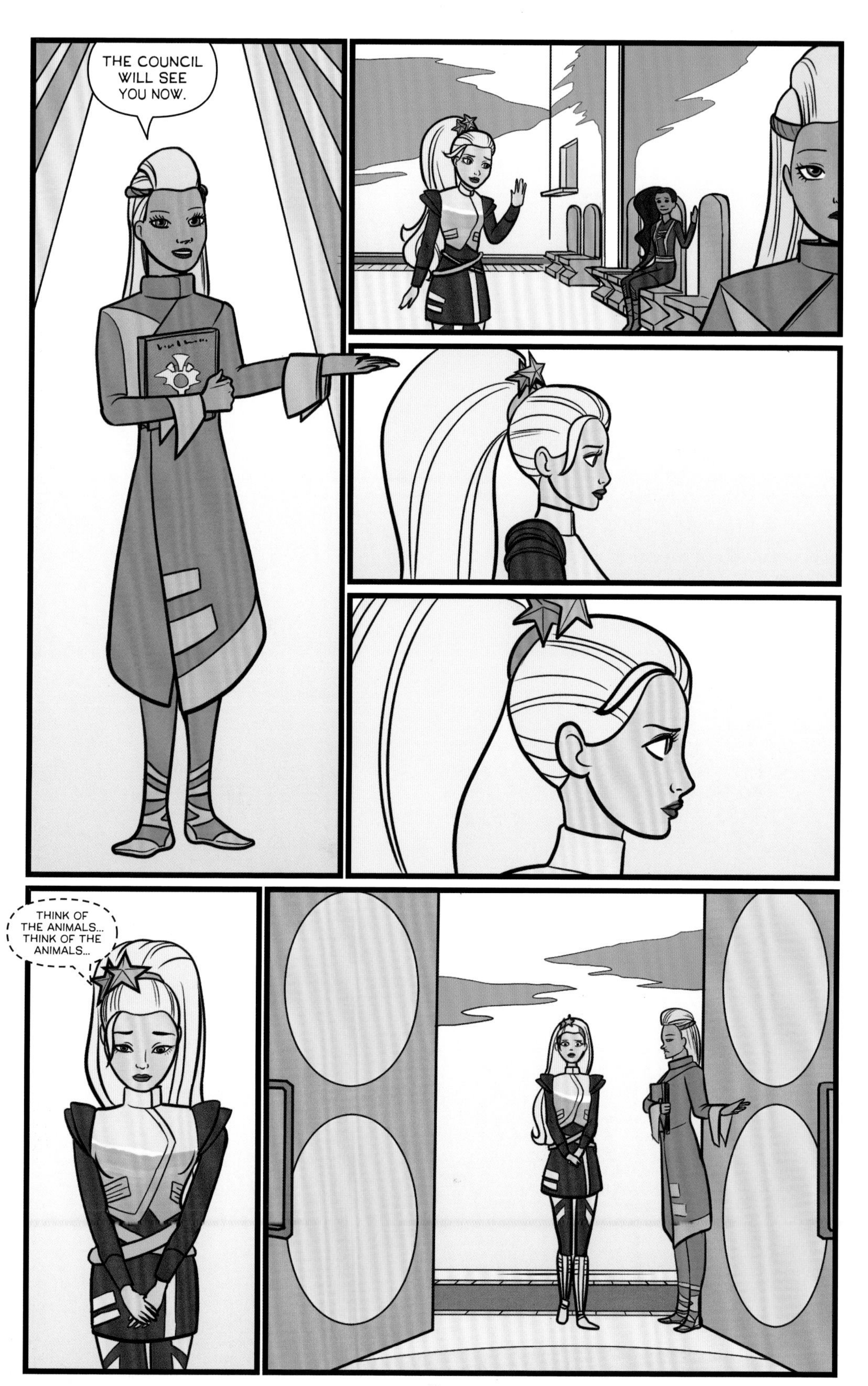
THE COUNCIL WILL SEE YOU NOW.
THINK OF THE ANIMALS... THINK OF THE ANIMALS...

OHH...
ENTER.

YOU MUST BE...PRINCESS STARLIGHT.
Y-YES, MA'AM.

OR AS YOUR FRIENDS CALL YOU, *BARBIE*.

YES, MA'AM. I--
YOU'RE RESPONSIBLE FOR THE RECENT DELAY TO STELLAR INDUSTRIES' PRODUCTION.

YES, MA'AM.

MS. STELLAR SENT US THESE IMAGES. BARBIE, WE'VE BEEN SO PROUD OF YOUR WORK ALL OVER THE GALAXY, BUT THIS JUST SEEMS... VERY UNLIKE YOU.
I CAN EXPLAIN.
SNRK
ELLA STELLAR SAID SHE'D BOUGHT THE LAND FROM THE COUNCIL, AND IT WAS HERS NOW. MY FRIENDS AND I DIDN'T BELIEVE HER--AND I'M SORRY FOR THAT. I JUST COULDN'T IMAGINE THAT YOU WOULD SELL OUR LAND FOR HER TO DESTROY LIKE THAT! NATURE IS SO IMPORTANT TO PARA-DEN.
DESTROY? MS. STELLAR SAID HER TEAM WAS *RESEARCHING* PARA-GEMS.
WELL, THAT MIGHT HAVE BEEN HER INTENTION AT FIRST, BUT NOW SHE'S ***MINING*** PARA-GEMS!

MINING?! BUT PARA-GEMS CAN'T BE MINED!
INDEED. WHERE THEY REALLY COME FROM IS A WELL-KEPT SECRET. BUT PERHAPS WE CAN SHARE THAT WITH BARBIE...
WE MUST CORRECT THIS MISUNDERSTANDING AT ONCE. BARBIE, WILL YOU HELP US?
OF COURSE!
WONDERFUL! BUT FIRST--WE HAVE SOMETHING TO SHARE WITH YOU.
I'M LISTENING...

LATER, BACK AT ELLA STELLAR'S WORK SITE...
I GOT IT!

I THINK THAT WAS THE LAST ONE WE NEED!
RUSTLE RUSTLE
WHAT DO YOU GUYS SAY? DOES THAT LOOK LIKE ENOUGH?

YOU MEAN IS IT ENOUGH TO--
--GET ELLA STELLAR'S ATTENTION?

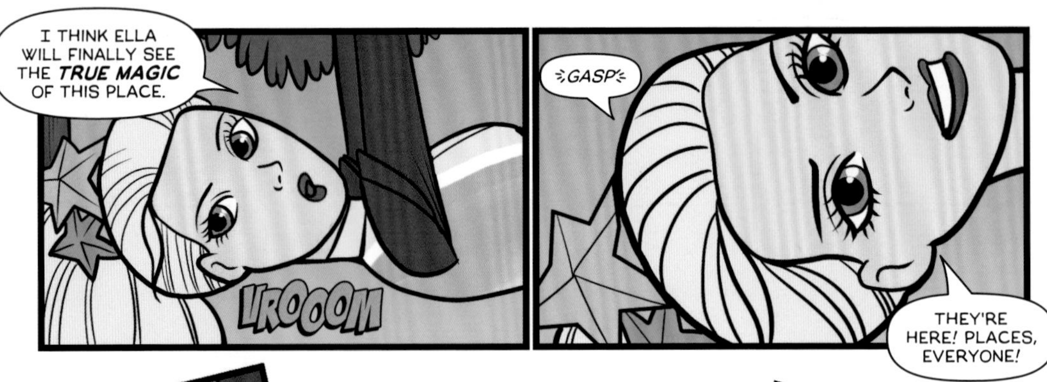
I THINK ELLA WILL FINALLY SEE THE **TRUE MAGIC** OF THIS PLACE.
VROOOM
GASP
THEY'RE HERE! PLACES, EVERYONE!

GOT MY HOVERBOARD!
YOU READY?
LET'S HIDE!

OKAY. READY.

BARBIE, I'M SURPRISED. I THOUGHT I MADE MYSELF CLEAR...
HELLO, ELLA. I HAVE SOMETHING IMPORTANT TO SHOW YOU.
THAT'S REALLY NICE, BUT...NO MATTER WHAT YOU HAVE TO SHOW ME, I HAVE A CONTRACT, REMEMBER?
THE GEMS AND EVERYTHING ELSE HERE BELONGS TO STELLAR INDUSTRIES.
PLEASE, JUST ONE MINUTE OF YOUR TIME.
FINE. 59 SECONDS LEFT.

HIT IT, SAL-LEE!

WHAT ARE YOU DOING? **NO!**
JUST WAIT, ELLA. YOU HAVEN'T SEEN **ANYTHING** YET!
YOU FOOLS!
THOSE ARE THE MOST IMPORTANT ENERGY SOURCE IN THE GALAXY-- YOU CAN'T JUST BURN THEM!

BOOM
BOOM
BOOM
NO!

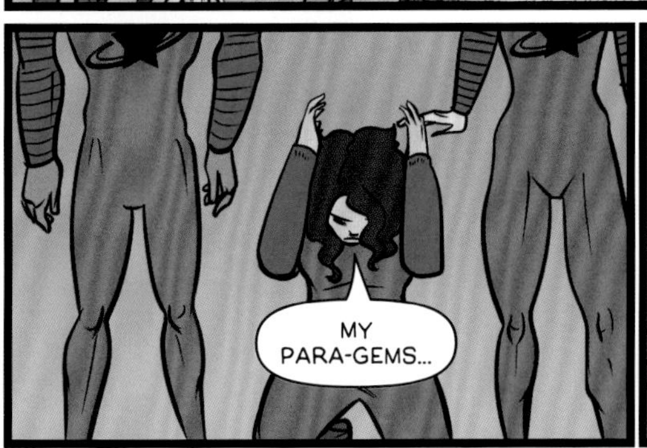
MY PARA-GEMS...

ONE MORE SECOND!

CREEEAAK

SEE? THEY'RE NOT STONES, THEY'RE SEEDS!
GASP

IF YOU TAKE ALL OF THEIR SEEDS OFFPLANET TO BURN AS FUEL, NO MORE TREES WILL GROW!
SO, WHAT, THEY JUST DROP OUT OF THE TREES, THEN?

YES! IF YOU'RE PATIENT.
SO LONG AS YOU CARE FOR THE FOREST AND TREAT THE TREES GENTLY INSTEAD OF JUST HACKING THEM ALL DOWN.

WHY DIDN'T YOU TELL ME THIS SOONER?

I THOUGHT SHOWING YOU THEIR MAGIC WOULD MAKE YOU TRULY UNDERSTAND.
IT'S PRETTY SCARY TO THINK SOMETHING THIS SPECIAL WAS ALMOST DESTROYED.

I COMPLETELY UNDERSTAND NOW. I'M SORRY WE WEREN'T HONEST WITH YOUR COUNCIL ABOUT WHAT WE PLANNED TO DO WITH THE PARA-GEMS. I SUPPOSE WE'RE NOT WELCOME HERE ANYMORE?

ON THE CONTRARY! THE COUNCIL AGREES THAT PARA-DEN CAN BE A GREAT TOURIST DESTINATION!

YEAH! HOVERBOARD RACES THROUGH THE WOODS...
AND SURFING--
--ON THE WAVES!

AND EXOTIC WILDLIFE!
ALL THINGS THAT REQUIRE THE PRESERVATION OF OUR AMAZING ECOSYSTEM!

ALL RIGHT, I GET IT. WE CHANGE OUR OPERATIONS FROM MINING TO...FARMING THESE THINGS?

THAT'S RIGHT! BE PATIENT, AND LOVE THE LAND, AND YOU'LL STILL BE ABLE TO USE SOME OF THE PARA-GEMS TO POWER YOUR SHIPS. AND WE CAN'T WAIT TO SEE EVERYONE WHO COMES TO VISIT!

HECK, BARBIE'S DAD WILL PROBABLY COOK FOR THEM!

WELL, YOUNG MAN, THAT'S A NICE THOUGHT, BUT THE STELLARSHIPS HOLD 500 PASSENGERS EACH...
OH...

...WE KNOW...

A FEW WEEKS LATER...
GEMBERRY DUMPLINGS! ON A STICK, OR SERVED ALONGSIDE OUR HAND-CHURNED FROZEN YOGURT! THEY'RE--WHAT IS IT, BARBIE?

...OUT OF THIS WORLD, DAD!
GROOOAAAN

OH! UM... ARE YOU HERE TO GET SOME DUMPLINGS?
I SURE AM! KEEPING THESE PARA-GEM TREES HAPPY IS HUNGRY WORK!

IT IS! GOOD THING WE'RE ALL READY TO HELP!
IT'S THE LAST DAY OF YOUR VACATION, ISN'T IT? DO YOUR FRIENDS MIND?

ARE YOU KIDDING? WITH OUR LAST DAY OF VISITING PARA-DEN--

--THERE'S NOTHING WE'D RATHER DO!
THE END.

WATCH OUT FOR PAPERCUTZ

Welcome to the fantasy-filled BARBIE STAR LIGHT ADVENTURE "The Secret of the Gems" graphic novel, by the fabulously futuristic team of Tini Howard, writer, and Jules Rivera, artist. We're thrilled that you're travelled to the farthest reaches of the galaxy to join Barbie on her latest exciting adventure.

If this is your first BARBIE graphic novel, you're in luck because there're two more BARBIE graphic novels also available that we're sure you'll just love!

The first graphic novel is BARBIE "Fashion Superstar." Barbie dreams of a career in fashion, and she just got her first big break—assisting world-famous fashion designer Whitney Yang at her big Spring Fashion Show! But when things start going wrong, it's up to Barbie and her friends to work some fashion miracles. Take a look at the preview starting on the very next page, to experience just a taste of this exciting graphic novel by Sarah Kuhn, writer, and Alitha Martinez, artist.

The second graphic novel is BARBIE PUPPY PARTY. Not only does it star Barbie, it also features Barbie's sisters, Chelsea, Stacie, and Skipper, along with their pet puppies, Honey, Rookie, Taffy, and DJ! The perplexed pooches suspect that the girls have forgotten about their birthday party when they see all the elaborate preparations going on for a party to adopt homeless pets. Can that possibly be the case? The answer awaits in BARBIE PUPPY PARTY!

But if you're a super-Barbie fan and already have these other two graphic novels, and you're looking for more fun graphic novels to enjoy while you're waiting for the next BARBIE novel to appear, may we suggest going to www.papercutz.com to check out some of the other great graphic novels we publish?

So, if you love BARBIE—either on Earth working as a fashion designer or with her sisters and puppies, or in outer space—or just fun, entertaining graphic novels with really cool characters—Papercutz has what you're looking for!

STAY IN TOUCH!

EMAIL: salicrup@papercutz.com
WEB: papercutz.com
TWITTER: @papercutzgn
FACEBOOK: PAPERCUTZGRAPHICNOVELS
FANMAIL: Papercutz, 160 Broadway, Suite 700 East Wing, New York, NY 10038

Special Preview of BARBIE #1
"Fashion Superstar"

ME, TOO! BUT, BARBIE... THE SHOW ISN'T UNTIL ***TOMORROW,*** RIGHT?
AND WE'LL BE READY FOR THAT, TOO, LIZ!
BUT RIGHT NOW, I'M READY TO SPEND ALL DAY CREATING THE ***PERFECT*** OUTFIT TO WEAR.
SO YOU'RE READY... *TO GET READY?*
EXACTLY.

I CAN'T BELIEVE I'M ASSISTING WHITNEY YANG AT HER BIG SPRING FASHION SHOW!
I'M GOING TO SEE HER LATEST CREATIONS, LEARN ALL ABOUT HOW A REAL DESIGNER WORKS...
I WILL BE LIKE A SPONGE, SOAKING IT ALL IN.
A KNOWLEDGE SPONGE. I LIKE IT.
AND I'LL BE RIGHT THERE WITH YOU, TAKING PHOTOS FOR THE STYLE LOVE BLOG!
YOUR INTERNSHIP IS GOING SO WELL! YOU'LL BE THEIR #1 FASHION PHOTOGRAPHER IN NO TIME!
I HOPE SO! THIS SHOW IS MY CHANCE TO REALLY PROVE MYSELF.
I FEEL THE SAME WAY. I WANT TO SHOW WHITNEY SHE MADE A GOOD CHOICE WHEN SHE PICKED ME OUT OF THE THOUSANDS OF PEOPLE WHO APPLIED FOR THE ASSISTANT JOB!
WE'RE IN THIS TOGETHER!
YES!

BUT WHY DO YOU HAVE TO CREATE A WHOLE NEW OUTFIT? YOU HAVE TONS OF AWESOME DESIGNS ALREADY.
THESE ARE JUST... THINGS I'VE MADE OVER THE YEARS. THEY'RE NICE, BUT THEY DON'T HAVE VISION.
HAVE... WHAT, NOW?

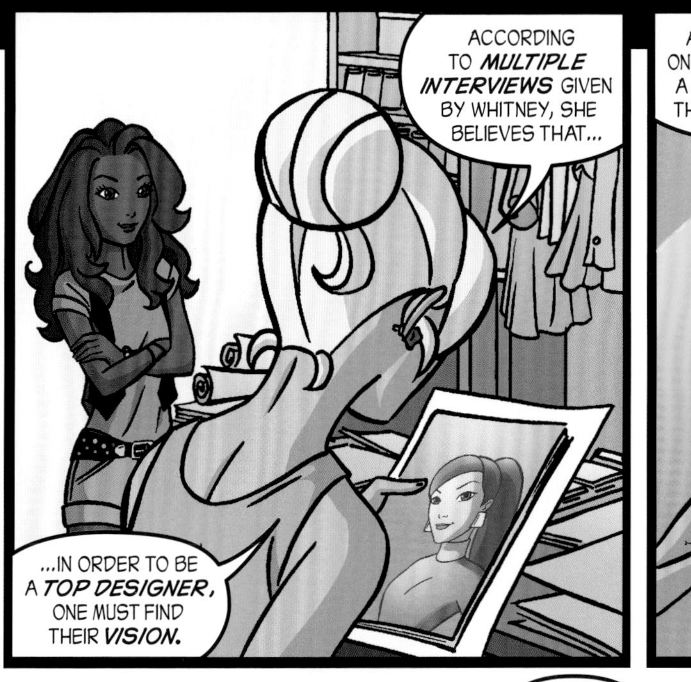
ACCORDING TO MULTIPLE INTERVIEWS GIVEN BY WHITNEY, SHE BELIEVES THAT...
...IN ORDER TO BE A TOP DESIGNER, ONE MUST FIND THEIR VISION.

AS SHE SAYS, VISION MEANS "THAT ONE BIT OF CREATIVITY THAT YOU, AS A UNIQUE DESIGNER, CAN PULL OFF. THE THING THAT ONLY YOU CAN DO."
I LOVE THAT WHITNEY IS SO CONFIDENT.

YES! SHE KNOWS WHO SHE IS AND ISN'T AFRAID TO EXPRESS HERSELF!
AND SHE'S RIGHT! I NEED TO FIND...

...MY VISION.
NO SLEEVE
NO
NO

I CAN DO THIS BY TOMORROW. I'VE READ EVERYTHING THERE IS TO READ ABOUT WHITNEY, I KNOW WHAT SHE LIKES, WHAT INSPIRES HER—
SHOULDN'T FINDING YOUR VISION BE ABOUT WHAT INSPIRES YOU?

THIS IS THE FIRST STEP IN ACHIEVING MY DREAM OF BECOMING A REAL FASHION DESIGNER.
AND WHITNEY'S MY HERO. SHE'S BEEN SHOWING FOR SIX SEASONS, AND HER DRESSES HAVE BEEN IN EVERY BIG FASHION MAGAZINE ON THE PLANET.
I HAVE TO IMPRESS HER.

WHAT ARE YOU DOING?
WHEN I NEED TO CREATE SOMETHING NEW, I DOODLE. IT HELPS ME *FOCUS*.
YOU DOODLE WITH... SPECIAL PAINT?
THE PAINTS ARE MY *CREATION*.
I'VE ALWAYS USED PAINT TO DOODLE-- BUT I DOODLE ON WHATEVER'S AROUND ME. SO I *EXPERIMENTED* UNTIL I CAME UP WITH A *CHEMICAL FORMULA* THAT WORKS ON *ANY SURFACE*.
SO YOU *INVENTED* THE SPECIAL PAINT?
SCIENCE IS AN IMPORTANT PART OF MY PROCESS.
I LIKE THIS *SCIENCE-ART MASHUP*. IT'S VERY *YOU*.
NOW LET ME LEAVE YOU WITH SOMETHING THAT'S VERY *ME*...

OOH, IS THAT A NEW PLAYLIST? YOUR PLAYLISTS ARE THE BEST!
YUP. ANOTHER "LIZ ORIGINALS" SET OF SELECTED TUNES.
MUSIC HELPS ME FOCUS ON MY PHOTOGRAPHY. LIKE DOODLING HELPS YOU FOCUS ON YOUR DESIGN. IT FUELS MY CREATIVITY.
YES! MY CREATIVITY FEELS MAJORLY FUELED. I'M READY! TO GET READY!
I CAN'T WAIT TO SEE WHAT YOU COME UP WITH!
I'M GOING TO GO DO SOME PRACTICE SHOTS WITH MY CAMERA!
AND WE'LL BOTH BE ACTUALLY READY TOMORROW AT 10 AM!

INTERESTING COLORS...
UNEXPECTED LAYERS...
WHIMSICAL SPARKLES...
EXCITING FABRICS...

OH! IT'S GETTING LATE. AND MY THOUGHTS AREN'T COMING TOGETHER. AM I TALKING TO MYSELF? I'M TALKING TO MYSELF.

TIME TO START CREATING.

BUT MY IDEAS AREN'T COMING TOGETHER EITHER.